I0530507

No

Christmas

WITHOUT

You

LaCricia A'ngelle

No Christmas Without You

Published by His Pen Publishing, LLC
Gadsden, Alabama 35907
www.hispenpublishing.com

Print ISBN: 978-1-944643-35-5

This book is also available in digital eBook format

DEDICATION:

ABOVE ALL OTHERS FATHER GOD, I GIVE YOU PRAISE!

To my loving family thank you for always loving
and supporting me.

Books by LaCricia A'ngelle

Girl, Naw!
It Ain't Over

Journey to Love
Worthy of Love

First Lady Series
Positive Deception
Lina's Redemption

Stand Alone Titles
The Christmas Gift (short story)

Young Adult
Sophomore Mom

CHAPTER 1

"Wake up Paul. Paul baby wake up. Please, baby, please wake up."

Tears raced down Dinah's cheeks as she held Paul's head in her arms. Her sobs could be heard throughout Owning's department store. Snatching several sweaters from a nearby rack, she pressed them into Paul's side desperately trying to stop the bleeding.

"Somebody, help," she yelled. Rubbing Paul's face, she kissed him on the top of his head. Paul looked at her with glassy eyes but didn't utter a word. "Hold on, baby. The ambulance is almost here. Please wake up, Paul. I love you baby, you can't leave me. God please, help. Don't let me lose him. God if you hear me, please stop the bleeding. Don't let Paul die," she cried in desperation.

Dinah's tears fell rapidly, collecting at the bottom of her chin before dropping onto Paul's forehead. EMTs rushed in with a gurney and medical bags.

"Ma'am we need you to step back," a young man urged, carefully pushing her aside as they began working on Paul.

Dinah reluctantly moved aside allowing the first responders to work on Paul. She watched in horror as everything felt surreal. How had they gone from an enjoyable shopping trip to this? Dinah prayed aloud begging the Lord to save her fiancé's life.

"God, please. I know you hear me, please don't let Paul die."

The EMTs cut Paul's shirt allowing access to his wound. One EMT packed the wound with gauze as the other hurriedly started an IV. They moved with quick, yet precise actions gently rolling Paul onto a backboard before lifting him onto the stretcher. Dinah ran behind them disregarding the bags filled with gifts she and Paul purchased prior to the shooting. Her crossbody handbag clung to her side.

The parking lot was filled with distraught shoppers, concerned family members, media, and law enforcement. The scene was controlled chaos. Blinded by tears, Dinah took a seat inside the ambulance by Paul's side. She reached out and took his hand as she mouthed a quiet prayer.

"Lord please let Paul live."

In agony, Dinah watched as an EMT rhythmically pumped oxygen into Paul's lungs by squeezing the small clear bag. Another technician started an IV. She held her breath and watched as his chest rose and fell showing her he was fighting.

Once Paul was taken care of, a paramedic turned to Dinah checking her for injuries. The seven minute ride to the hospital felt endless. Although everyone around her was moving with rapid calculated movements, Dinah felt as if she herself was moving in slow motion. Arriving at the hospital she was escorted to the waiting room despite her protest. She felt helpless as she watched the man she hoped to spend the rest of her life with be wheeled to the back surrounded by hospital personnel.

Chapter 2

With shaky hands, Dinah pulled her phone from her purse. Splatters of blood on her purse and clothes reminded her of the reason she was sitting in the uncomfortable chair in the cold, sterile waiting room. Her first call was to Paul's mother, Florence. She struggled to pull herself together enough to inform Florence of Paul's condition. Tapping her foot incessantly she recounted the shooting and hospital information to Paul's mother.

"I'm on my way," Florence declared before disconnecting the call.

Without delay, Dinah called her own mother. Unable to hold back the emotion any longer she let loose as soon as she heard her mother's voice on the phone.

"Mommy," she cried with heart wrenching sobs.

"Dinah what's wrong?" Her mother asked matching her tone.

"It's...it's Paul. He's been shot. We're at the hospital.

"Shot?" How? Where?"

"Oh, Mommy it's bad. They won't let me see him.

"Where are you, baby?"

"Balsam General. I'm in the emergency waiting room. I'm covered in blood but I can't leave."

"Why didn't they check you out? Are you sure you weren't shot?"

"Yes, I'm sure. The EMTs checked me out while we were in the ambulance." Dinah fell silent for a moment. "I don't know what I'll do if I lose Paul. Mommy he's my everything."

"Baby, try to calm down. I know it's hard but you have to pull yourself together so you can think rationally. You have some clothes here. I'll grab something for you and head over to the hospital. I'll get there as quick as I can."

"Thank you," Dinah sobbed into the phone.

"Pray, baby. Just pray. God is able to do anything. I'll be there soon. I love you, Dinah."

"I love you too."

Removing the phone from her ear, Dinah placed the device back inside her purse. She clasped her hands together, bowed her head and prayed.

"Where is my baby?"

Dinah snapped her eyes open and turned in the direction of the screechy voice. She blinked back tears as Florence rushed over to her laced in hysteria.

"Oh my God, is that his blood?" Florence wailed drawing the attention of everyone in the waiting room.

Standing, Dinah pulled Florence into an embrace and with care guided her to the seat next to hers. With strength she didn't realize she had, Dinah struggled to control her emotions in order to comfort Paul's dejected mother. Holding her close she allowed Florence to cry until she was spent.

Florence pulled away and sat upright. "Dinah, baby what happened? I spoke with Paul a little while ago and he was fine. How did this happen, who shot him? Why would anyone want to hurt my baby?"

"I asked myself the same question a hundred times but the truth is Paul was a victim. There's no other explanation. Last night he told me he wanted to go today to pick up his groomsmen's gifts and to get some other stuff for the wedding, so we went. We were done shopping and heading out the store when out of nowhere we heard rapid gunfire. We tried to take cover and that's when Paul fell." Dinah tried to continue but her words were replaced with sobs.

The people in the waiting room began clearing out one by one leaving Dinah and Florence. Joyce arrived carrying a small bag with a change of clothing for Dinah. Dinah refused to go change out of fear of missing the doctor.

Hours passed further increasing the ladies anxiety. They

4

alternated between praying collectively aloud and individual inward petitions.

"Cheatham family?" the doctor called out standing in the doorway of the waiting room.

"I'm Mrs. Cheatham," Florence said, pushing herself toward him. Dinah on her heels.

With bated breath they stood in front of the doctor. He removed his surgical cap, looked at them and dropped his head.

CHAPTER 3

Dinah stared out the window, watching the small white flakes fall to the ground joining the growing accumulation of freshly fallen snow. It was the first real snowfall of the season. The bitter cold dropped the ground temperature enough for the light dusting to lay uniform without melting. Rooftops and evergreens served as eloquent props allowing the powdery fluff to take center stage.

Using both hands, Dinah gripped the mug filled with hot chocolate and a massive number of mini marshmallows. Licking the mug, she savored the sweet taste of melted marshmallow cascading down the side. A smile creased her lips as she focused on the image of her and Paul wearing Santa hats displayed on the side of the mug.

Paul had given her the mug three years prior as a gag gift for Christmas. She grimaced recalling the noticeable disappointment in Paul's eyes when he discovered she was more excited about the mug than the diamond teardrop earrings he had purchased for her. Dinah spent over an hour trying to convince Paul she did in fact like the earrings, but the mug held a deeper value for her. From that day forward, Dinah used the mug daily.

Fierce yelling penetrated the walls pulling Dinah from her recollecting. Turning her head in the direction of the noise, Dinah rolled her eyes. *Why can't these people get it together? I get so sick of them arguing and fighting.* "Just toxic," Dinah declared aloud. Rising from the sofa she picked up a remote, powered the television on and increased the volume. She would rather listen to reruns of old television programs than to hear her neighbors at each other's throats again.

Vibrations rippled through her vinyl couch cushions alerting her of an incoming call on her cell phone. With swift movements Dinah grabbed the phone and slid her finger across the screen accepting the call before it transferred to voicemail. A distraction was exactly what she needed. The robotic voice elicited and immediate eye roll when Dinah realized the caller was nothing more than a computerized solicitation.

The bickering coming from next door grew louder. She knew if she stayed in the living room she wouldn't be able to relax. Taking a long swallow on her way into the kitchen, Dinah resisted the urge to spit the now cool liquid back into the mug. She rolled her eyes before placing the mug in the sink.

Reflecting on the fresh snowfall, Dinah snapped her fingers. She figured she'd better head to the store to grab a few things before the weather conditions worsened. Dinah moved over to the refrigerator and retrieved her grocery list from a magnetic note pad. Over the past two years her compulsive planning had intensified. She was very meticulous, being careful not to leave out any detail. Planning gave her a feeling of control. The thought of leaving anything important to chance unnerved her. After a final assessment of her fridge and pantry, she scurried into the bedroom to retrieve her purse.

12:17 PM displayed on her wristwatch. A trip to the grocery store was the only errand on her agenda for the day. She figured the hustle and bustle of the grocery store would be better than the sound of bickering coming from the neighbors. Dinah moved to the closet and retrieved her outerwear. Stomping, she forced her foot into a pair of tan boots before pulling her matching parka onto her shoulders. Although there was only a little snow, the cold temperature was bitter. Dinah placed a wool scarf crocheted by her grandmother loosely around her neck. Catching a cold or worse, the flu was not on her agenda.

Dinah scrambled through her purse until she recovered her keys. In times past the presence of snow increased the number of shoppers in the store adding to her anxiety. Pausing, she considered the option of having her grocery delivered or using the store's grocery pickup service. Dinah dismissed the idea. She'd fought hard to regain a sense of normalcy and the confidence to go out in public following the shooting. She couldn't afford to regress.

Customers packed the grocery store filling their baskets with essentials and items Dinah was certain were ingredients for holiday meals.

"Merry Christmas, Miss. Would you like a sugar cookie? We bake and decorate them here in the store. I happen to know they are Santa's personal favorite." The small framed woman smiled brightly extending a tray of cookies to Dinah. Deep wrinkles appearing like parentheses framed her mouth and eyes.

"No thank you," Dinah said holding up her hand to deter the woman from further approach.

"We also have delicious cakes and pies that can round out your holiday meal.

"No, thank you." Dinah stated exaggerating each word.

The woman's expression changed from cheer to one of pity. "You have a blessed day, dear. I hope the good Lord blesses you with your heart's desire this Christmas."

Dinah rolled her eyes and pushed her basket past the woman heading toward the frozen food section. The thought of preparing a Christmas dinner brought memories she wasn't prepared to deal with. Christmas dinner for her would be much like every other dinner which consisted of whichever frozen meal was on sale.

"What's up, Cousin," Jonesha called out from the end of the aisle.

Dinah turned towards the familiar voice. Smiling she extended her arms and pulled her cousin in for a hug. "Hey, girl. What are you up to?"

"Nothing. Just trying to get the last of my shopping done for Christmas dinner. I talked to your sister Jacquie the other day and she said Auntie has a big dinner planned. I told her I can bring a couple cheesecakes. You know she jumped all over that because folks be loving my cheesecakes." Jonesha gushed.

"Your cheesecakes are delicious, I'll have to give it to you."

"Don't be trying to sneak one out when you get to Auntie's house. Coming up in there with a whole set of storage containers." Jonesha laughed at her quick wit.

8

"Okay, I see you got jokes, Jonesha. Don't worry your cheesecakes will be safe. I'm probably not going to be there anyway."

Suddenly distracted, Jonesha reached into Dinah's shopping basket and flipped through the assortment of frozen meals. "Girl, how many frozen dinners you got in that basket? Dang, Cuz, are you shopping or stocking? Open that coat, I know you got a blue apron on under there. Where's your nametag?"

"Stop playing, Jonesha. You know good and well I don't work here. I like these dinners. They're easy and they taste good. I'm not trying to cook for one person. That's crazy."

"Hold up, and back up. I know I got off the subject, but did you say you're not going to Christmas dinner at your own mama's house or did I make that up in my mind? Cause if you did say it, you have got to be crazy.

"Yes, I said it. I plan to get some rest on Christmas. I'm going to enjoy that extra day off. One of these dinners will work fine."

"Now I know good and well Aunt Joyce is gone be cooking her butt off. Why aren't you going over there."

Dinah rolled her eyes, she wasn't in the mood to debate Christmas with her cousin. For the past two years she found herself in a constant battle with her family and the few friends she had left over her decision not to celebrate Christmas.

"Don't ask questions you already know the answer to, Jo. I'm not about to go there with you."

"You don't have to go there. I'm not trying to argue with you. I don't have time for the negative energy. I will say this though, it's been two years, don't you think it's about time for you to get over it and move on?" At this point not even Paul would blame you. I'm not trying to be insensitive but you trippin." Jonesha threw her arm around Dinah's shoulder as if their conversation hadn't become heated.

Stepping away from her cousin, Dinah gripped her shopping basket firmly. "I don't have time for this."

Frustrated by Dinah's reaction, Jonesha spat, "I'm telling you the truth and you know it. Everybody else is walking on eggshells trying to keep from hurting your feelings, but I love you too much to lie to you. You don't go no where. Shoot, you even started working from home just so you don't have to see people. Girl, that is not no way to live."

"Bye, Jonesha," Dinah huffed pushing her shopping basket past her cousin. Her eyes burned as unshed tears threatened to make their escape.

Without another word exchanged, Dinah moved away from her cousin. She was so sick of people telling her how she should feel. Paul had only been gone for two years. Why people felt they had a right to tell her how long to grieve was beyond her imagination. Paul was the love of her life and her husband to be. Their marriage was supposed to take place on Christmas day. Instead of a wedding, she had to prepare for a funeral. Dinah still believed in God, but she didn't understand how He could allow someone as kind and loving as Paul to be taken away in such a violent manner.

The thought of interacting with another person was more than Dinah wanted to deal with. Maneuvering her way through the maze of people, she pushed her shopping basket to the self-checkout, completed her purchase, and exited the store as quickly as she could.

The wheels on the shopping basket squeaked in tune with the sound of snow crushing underneath Dinah's booties. Feelings of sadness were quickly being replaced with those of anger and frustration. Who or what gave Jonesha the right to come for her like that. Dinah was sick of people's opinions. Feeling like they had the right to tell her how to feel and how long to mourn.

A cold wind whipped around Dinah causing her teeth to chatter. Opening the trunk to her vehicle, she tossed the bags inside and quickly climbed into the driver's seat. Dinah clasped her hands together and blew a warm breath into the hollow space while she waited impatiently for her car to heat up.

A box of tissues positioned on the front passenger seat sat ready to dispense the soft cloths prepared to soak up the flood of tears staining Dinah's face. Snatching several tissues from the box, Dinah dabbed at her eyes. She gripped the steering wheel with such fervor it caused her hands to ache. She missed Paul constantly but the Christmas season was hardest for her. They both had loved Christmas and everything related to it.

Dinah dried her tears and took a deep breath. As much as she wished she could change things, she knew she couldn't. Paul was gone and he wasn't coming back. She knew in her heart tear filled days are not what he would have wanted for her, but she couldn't help it. Dinah forced a slight chuckle when she thought about the look Paul would give her when he felt like she was overreacting or if he wanted her to get past something. He would tilt his head toward her, raise his eyebrow and buck his eyes causing her to laugh.

Starting the car, Dinah adjusted the heat and backed out of the parking space. "You got this, girl," she said aloud while peeping at herself in the rearview mirror. If she could manage to get past the holiday season she knew she would be okay.

CHAPTER 4

"Mama, I wanna go outside," Cash said tapping his mother on her leg.

"Don't you see me on the phone," Gina barked turning briefly as she lowered the phone to her side.

"Please, mama. I wanna build a snowman."

"Gone then, I don't care. Put a coat on and don't leave from out front of the building." Gina returned to her call without taking a second glance at her six year old son.

"Okay,"

Cash ran full speed until he reached the closet located near the door to their apartment. He stood on tip toes and tugged on the bottom of his coat until it fell free from the hanger. He pulled his coat on and darted out the door. Stepping outside, Cash looked at the snow and grinned. With outstretched hands he allowed the flakes to touch his bare palms before melting.

Climbing down the concrete steps, being careful not to slip, Cash made his way to the ground. He kneeled down and gathered a handful of snow. Cash rubbed his hands together and created a small snowball. He continued gathering snow until he had three snowballs of various sizes. Moving over to the step he placed the snowballs on top of each other creating a tiny snowman. Cash stepped over to the yard and kicked the small blanket of snow around in search of a twig he could break in half to use for arms.

Dinah pulled up to the curb, parked her car and turned the engine off. She climbed out the car, opened the trunk, and gathered the bags filling each arm with the thin handles of the plastic shopping bags.

"I can help you. I'm a big boy," Cash proclaimed drawing Dinah's attention downward.

"That's okay, baby. I've got it." Dinah replied disregarding the offer.

"No you don't. You can't even close the trunk." Cash said pointing to the open trunk door. "Let me help, please."

"Little boy, don't you know you're not supposed to talk to strangers? What's your name?" she asked.

"Cash, and I'm a big boy not a little boy," he replied trying to sound intimidating. "Annnnd," He said dragging the word out. "You're not a stranger. We live in the same building next door to each other, so you can't be a stranger if we live in the same place."

"We may live in the same place, but I am still a stranger."

"Your name is Cash?" Dinah asked again in disbelief.

"That's what I said. Cash. My mama named me Cash because she said I'm gon' be getting paid when I grow up."

"If you keep running up on strangers the way you're doing you might not get to grow up. Some people are not right in the head and they will hurt you."

"Please, can I help you?" Cash interjected, ignoring Dinah's chastening. "That's a lot of bags and you still have to be able to get inside. How you gonna turn the doorknob if your hands are full. I bet you didn't think about that."

Realizing she wasn't going to win, Dinah accepted Cash's offer. "Okay, Cash. By the way, my name is Dinah. You can help me take the bags inside the building but only to my apartment door."

"Okay," Cash clapped his hands and grabbed two of the bags from Dinah. He led Dinah into the building.

"Watch out for my snowman," Cash said as they approached the steps.

"That little thing? It can't be a snowman, it's too small." Dinah replied.

"Yes it can. Just cause it's small right now don't mean nothing. You want to know why Miss. Dinah?"

"Yes. Why?"

"Because I'm gone keep adding more snow to it and it's gonna get bigger and bigger." Cash stretched his arms out with a grocery bag in each hand emphasizing his point. "I have to protect him while he's small but when he get's big everybody will be able to see him."

Dinah looked at the little boy walking before her with genuine astonishment. She wondered if he figured he was just talking or if he actually knew the magnitude of wisdom he had spoken.

The two arrived at Dinah's apartment. Cash placed the bags on the floor outside the door. He looked up at Dinah and gave her a wide grin.

"See, Miss Dinah, I told you I could do it. Told you I'm a big boy."

"Yes, you did." Dinah reached into her pocket and pulled out a dollar wrapped up in a receipt. She pulled the receipt away and handed the money to Cash. "Thank you for your help."

Cash grabbed the money and stuffed it into his pocket. "Thank you, Miss Dinah. I woulda helped you for free though." Holding up the dollar, he said, "I'm taking this to the store." Cash ran to his apartment door, quickly turned the knob, and stepped inside.

"Mama. I got some money."

Dinah picked up the bags and made her way into the apartment. Taking her time, she packed the frozen dinners neatly into the freezer. Her mind easily drifted to the little boy from next door. On numerous occasions Dinah had seen Cash playing outside, but she never knew he was her neighbor's child.

Rolling her eyes in disgust, Dinah thought about the constant arguing and sound of unruly behavior that often penetrated the wall she shared with her neighbor. She didn't want to think about what all little Cash may have been exposed to. Dinah couldn't help but smile at the thought of Cash's chubby face and dimples so deep he could hide dimes in them. Releasing the breath, she didn't realize she had been holding, Dinah shook her head and shifted her focus. Dwelling on something totally unrelated to her was a waste of time. On the other hand, Dinah was grateful. If nothing else, Cash was a welcomed distraction from her previous interaction with her cousin.

CHAPTER 5

Startled awake by the sound of her ringing cell phone, Dinah's heart pounded. She had finally fallen into a deep sleep after drinking a cup of chamomile tea the night prior. The interaction with her cousin at the grocery store caused Dinah's mind to go into overdrive with thoughts of Paul. She wrestled with feelings of guilt. Why hadn't she tried to discourage Paul from going shopping that day? Why did they choose Owning's? There were plenty of other stores they could have patronized. One small decision had robbed Paul of his life and had forever changed Dinah's life.

The phone rang once again rescuing Dinah from the bottomless pit of guilt she was once again heading into. Grabbing the phone from her bedside table she answered groggily.

"Hello."

"Dinah. Girl, I know you're not still asleep. It's almost noon. What are you doing over there?"

"Yes, Mama. I was still asleep," Dinah sighed in frustration. "I was up late because I couldn't sleep, so I drank some chamomile tea."

"Don't you think it's about time for you to get up now? Jonesha told me she saw you at the grocery store. She said you were talking about not coming over here for Christmas dinner and then you got mad when she said something to you about it."

"I'm sure that's all she told you too. Jonesha is good at telling a one sided story to make herself sound all innocent. She came at me sideways and rather than go off on her like she deserved, I chose to walk away.

"She told me something about telling you it's time for you to move on past Paul. Humph, girl you have got to stop letting everything get to you. I can't say she's wrong, but knowing Jonesha

15

the way I do, I'm sure her approach could have been better."

"I don't mean any harm, Mama but I need to know. Is this what y'all do, sit around talking about me and how I need to get over Paul?"

"Wait a minute, Dinah."

"Mama, I'm sorry. I really don't mean any disrespect. This is not easy. I thought if anyone would have my back it would be you. You know what this time of year does to me. How am I supposed to just get over the fact that instead of planning anniversary events and celebrating with my husband, I'm constantly reminded of his death? Every time I see a commercial for Owning's department store my mind is forced back to the day Paul died. Do you know how many times I have replayed that day in my mind wondering why he got shot and not me. Why he's gone and I'm still here?"

"You're still here because God has a purpose for your life. Your work here on earth is not done. Baby, please understand, it's not that we don't care. We're your family and we love you. We only want the best for you. Closing yourself off from everybody and sulking in your grief all season long is not healthy. Despite the circumstances." Her mother sighed in exasperation. "You had counseling before, I'm think you need to consider going back. You can't continue to live like this Dinah."

Dinah reached over and outlined Paul's face on the photo resting on her bedside table. Tears burned her eyes.

"Mama, I can't do this right now. I'll call you later." Dinah disconnected the call before her mother could protest.

Pushing back the covers, Dinah slid her legs around and eased out of the bed headed straight for the shower. Turning the water on as hot as she could stand it, she stood under the scorching spray. Sulking in a stream of sorrow, her tears flowed in unison with the water. Dinah didn't bother adjusting the heat feeling nothing could hurt her any more than the grief she was experiencing. She was not in the mood to deal with drama another day. Her heart ached as if it was being pulled from her chest. It didn't matter to her how long Paul had been gone. The memories of that horrible day replayed in her mind as if the shooting had just happened. She didn't know how much more she could take. The bathroom filled with steam in response to the intense heat from the water.

Dinah remained under the water until the hot water tank exhausted its contents causing the water to turn cold. Toweling off, she returned to her bedroom and dressed in a warmup suit. She desperately needed a distraction one she hoped her daily dose of TV cooking shows would provide.

Chapter 6

Dinah filled a mug with coffee and made her way to the living room. She noticed a gap in her curtains. Realizing she had left the curtain opened the day before, Dinah moved to the window to close them. Her eyebrows furrowed etching a deep wrinkle in her forehead. Slamming her mug down on the coffee table, Dinah rushed outside.

"Cash, what are you doing out here?"

"I'm building another snowman. Some stupid dummy kicked my other one down." Cash replied forcing his words through his missing two front teeth.

"Don't be talking like that. Get in this building." Dinah grabbed the little boy by the hand pulling him into the building.

Cash initially resisted but relinquished his fight when he saw the serious expression on Dinah's face. Once inside he pulled his hand from Dinah's grasp.

Dinah looked down at the little boy and squinted her eye. She didn't attempt to grab his hand again since they were safely inside.

Arriving in front of his apartment door, Dinah hit the door with rapid taps.

"Who is it?" a female voice called from the other side.

"Dinah, your neighbor." She heard the sound of locks being turned before the door swung open.

"What's up?" a petite young woman who appeared to be no more than twenty-two years old answered.

Moving him forward by his shoulder, Dinah pushed the little boy toward the woman. "Your son was outside playing in the snow with no coat on. He's going to get sick."

The young woman reached down and pulled Cash into the apartment the rest of the way. "Boy, what is you doing outside with no coat on? It's cold out there. When your stupid butt get sick don't

18

expect me to take you to the doctor."

"Wait a minute, I know I heard you unlocking the door before you opened it. Did you really lock him out? Anything could have happened to him besides the fact he didn't have on a coat," Dinah snapped.

"First of all, I didn't know he was outside. He was supposed to be watching TV. I can't watch him every minute."

"Are you freaking kidding me? This little boy is what, five years old?"

"He's six."

"It doesn't matter. He was outside long enough to almost build an entire snowman. Not to mention the fact he wasn't wearing a coat. It ain't nothing you could have been doing so important that you wouldn't notice you were missing a kid."

"Don't worry about what I was doing. How about you mind your own business and get away from my door," the young woman said closing the door in Dinah's face.

Dinah stepped away from the door pissed. *The nerve of her closing the door and dismissing me like I was nothing,* she thought. Dinah had as much as she could stand. She stepped away before her anger got the best of her. She entered her apartment and slammed the door behind.

Rushing into the bedroom, Dinah dove onto the bed planting her face in the pillow. She screamed from the depths of her inner being. The pillow muffled the sound but did little to absorb the pain. These were the moments Dinah fought hard to conceal. Moments when she was left alone with her thoughts which felt like a terroristic interrogation.

She continued to scream into the pillow filling it with the moisture of tears and drool. Her thoughts ran rampant. What was the point of her life? Why was she still alive? Why did Paul alone get shot when they had been standing together. Dinah went back and forth. She often wished she had suffered the same fate as Paul. At least then, she wouldn't be left behind to suffer the pain of losing him. *Where was God in all of this*, she wondered.

In her mind, there was nothing else to live for. The love of her life was gone, there was no other man she could ever desire. Her life felt like it was falling apart and she had no one to help pick up the pieces. Those that were supposed to be closest to her only criticized her, telling her to get over it. They minimized her pain, yet wondered why she avoided them.

"That's it. God, if you're really there then I need you to show me because I can't live like this." Throwing her hands in the air, Dinah declared, "What's the use it's not like you listen to my prayers any way." Rising from the bed she violently wiped her face dry and returned to the kitchen. It was time for her to end the pain once and for all.

CHAPTER 7

Incessant banging on her apartment door roused Dinah from a deep sleep. She opened her eyes and struggled to survey her surroundings in the dark room. Wincing in pain she grabbed her neck hoping to massage away the ache in her neck and shoulder. The banging continued. Sitting up, Dinah attempted to stand. Her head ached and a wave of nausea threatened to send her running to the bathroom. She tripped over an empty bottle of vodka causing her to stubble to the door. The repeated banging sounded like bombs being dropped in her apartment. The pain in her head prevented her from yelling stop to the pesky visitor on the other side of the door.

"Who is it?" she called out once she reached the door.

The knocking continued.

Dinah snatched open the door ready to pounce on whoever it was banging on her door like they were crazy.

Cash stood at the door with a tear streaked face.

"What in the world are you doing banging on my door like this. Where is your mama? What time is it?" Dinah looked back into the apartment and squinted to see the time on the microwave. "Boy, it's after two o'clock in the morning."

Tears formed once again in the little boy's eyes. His chest heaved as he fought off heavy sobs. "I'm scared and my mama ain't home. Can I come over here with you Miss Dinah?"

"What?" Dinah asked in disbelief.

"I heard somebody outside my window. They sound like they was about to break in. I was scared so I ran to my mama room, but she ain't there. I looked all over but she not nowhere in there," Cash said looking toward his apartment door.

"Come on in here," Dinah said stepping aside. She flicked the light switch on the wall illuminating the living room.

"It stink in here," Cash said attempting to cover his nostrils with his upper lip.

"I could always send your little behind back to your apartment."

"Noooooo. I'm sorry. Please don't make me go back over there by myself," Cash replied.

Dinah retrieved the empty bottle from the floor and placed it in the garbage container next to the kitchen counter. She returned to the living room and found Cash sitting on the sofa she had just vacated.

"Where is your mother?" She asked taking a seat across from him. "What in the world are you doing home alone, especially at this hour."

"I don't know where my mama is, Miss Dinah. She go out sometimes and leave me at home. I told you I'm a big boy. My mama said I'm a big boy and big boys can stay home by they self. She only go when it's time for me to go to bed and when I wake up, she always be back. This time I got scared so I woke up early." Cash looked at Dinah with eyes filled with innocence. "Can I stay here until she get home? I promise I won't mess with nothing."

"Yeah, I guess you can. There's no way I'm sending you back over there alone." She rose from the chair and approached Cash. "Here, stretch out and try to get some sleep." Dinah pulled a throw blanket from the back of the sofa and placed it over Cash. "I'm going to leave a note for your mama letting her know you're here so she can get you when she gets home."

Dinah pulled open the drawer in the end table and grabbed a pen and notepad. She scribbled *Your son is at my house. He was afraid. I need to talk to you when you come get him. Your next door neighbor, Dinah.* Dinah folded the paper in half, walked over to her neighbor's apartment, and placed the note by the doorknob where it was sure to be found. She returned to the apartment and found Cash sleeping soundly. Although Cash's arrival at her door was sobering, it didn't assuage her headache.

With quiet steps she went to her bathroom for aspirin. Dinah stared at her reflection. The woman with bloodshot eyes, tousled hair, and dried drool leading from her mouth to her cheek staring back at her was a woman Dinah didn't recognize. Grabbing a towel off the shelf next to her sink, Dinah washed her face and scooped water with her hand taking sips until she felt the aspirin tablets slide down her throat.

In the kitchen, Dinah made a single cup of black coffee. Although induced by alcohol, she was grateful for the hours of sleep she had gotten earlier. She returned to the living room and sat down on the chair. She wanted to make sure she was wide awake when Cash's mother came home. Dinah looked over at the sleeping child and shook her head. She thought, *this is going to be a long night.*

CHAPTER 8

"Miss Dinah, I'm hungry. Do you have some cereal? I can fix it myself if you tell me where it is."

Dinah glanced up at the clock in confusion. 8:20 AM read on the display. She undoubtedly had fallen asleep once again. Cash standing before her anticipating her response was proof the events of last night were not just an alcoholic illusion. Her neighbor's kid really was in her apartment.

"Hold up. If you're still here, that means either your mother has not come home yet, or she did come home and ignored my note for her to come get you."

Dinah bolted out of the apartment and headed for her neighbor's door. She noticed the note tucked in the same position she had left it in. For good measure, she approached the door and knocked until she was sure no one was inside. Returning to the apartment she found Cash sitting on the sofa staring at his hands.

"Does your mama always stay gone this long, Cash?"

"I don't think so. She always use to be home when I wake up. My stomach 'bout to growl. Can I have something to eat. I know you got some food because I helped you bring the bags in the other day. I'd rather have cereal or some breakfast food, but I'll eat one of them TV dinners you bought if that's all you got."

"Boy." Dinah wanted to fuss but she couldn't help but laugh. Cash's expression was one of both innocence and sincerity. "I'm sure there's something in here for you to eat. Come on."

Dinah watched as Cash ate his cereal and laughed at the cartoons she turned on for him. His laughter filled the apartment. She couldn't understand how anyone could neglect the poor child, but she was not ignorant to the fact that many parents and caregivers did the same thing every day.

A news clip flashed on the screen giving details of the overnight snowstorm that hit blanketing the city with ten inches of snow. Dinah dropped down on the sofa. She rationalized the snow being the reason for Cash's mother not returning.

Dinah grabbed her cell phone. "Cash, do you know your mother's cell phone number? I'm going to call her."

Cash took the phone from Dinah and keyed the numbers in without hesitation. He was met with a robotic voice. *The number you have dialed is temporarily not in service.* "It don't work. Mama probably changed her number again. She change it all the time. She said she be tired of stupid people calling her."

"Is there someone else we can call?" Dinah asked. "Perhaps a grandparent, aunt, or uncle?"

Handing the phone back to Dinah, Cash answered, "My grandmama lives far away and I don't have her phone number anyway. I don't have no auntie or uncle that I know of."

"I see." Dinah took the phone from Cash. "Did you leave your apartment door unlocked last night when you came over here?"

"I don't know. I was so scared I ran out of there like the Flash." Cash jumped up and ran around the room demonstrating his speed.

"Okay, I get it. Please stop running before you break something. You need to put on clean clothes and to brush your teeth. Let's go see if the door is unlocked."

CHAPTER 9

The day was almost gone and there was still no sign of Cash's mother. Dinah did her best to keep him entertained. She was surprised to see how comfortable Cash was being alone with her. They spent the day playing games, watching television, and they even went outside and built a new snowman. Dinah found herself laughing, something she hadn't done around this time of year in a long time.

She was glad Cash had left his apartment door open. They were able to get everything he needed including his hat and gloves. After getting the necessary items, Dinah returned the note to the door in case Cash's mother returned home.

After dinner, Dinah decided to treat him to a snack of hot chocolate and graham crackers. Dinah filled the mugs and put the sweet crackers on a saucer. After placing the items on a tray, she carried them into the living room and sat the tray down on the coffee table.

Cash lit up with excitement. "That's Mr. Paul," he exclaimed pointing to Paul's picture on Dinah's mug.

Dinah's hands shook. Taking a deep breath to steady herself, Dinah asked, "How do you know Paul?"

"Mr. Paul used to be my friend," Cash answered nonchalantly before taking a bite of his graham cracker. "He used to talk to me all the time and sometimes give me candy when he saw me outside playing. Mr. Paul was real nice. I was little but I still remember him. I would be outside and when he went to get in his car he always said *hey little man, you're a special kid and you gone do big things in the world. Make every day count. Life is precious.* I said yes Mr. Paul I will. He said it so much I learned it so when he would start saying it, I finished it. Man, he used to crack up when I did that." Cash blew into the hot chocolate to cool it off before taking a sip. "I haven't seen him in a long time though. I thought he moved, but mama said she saw on the news something happened to him and now he in heaven. I miss Mr. Paul, he was cool."

Dinah sat dazed. She recalled Paul constantly buying candy to add to her candy dish even though he rarely ate any. Sometimes when he would leave going home, he'd grab a few pieces out of the dish and say this is for my little friend. Dinah never thought to ask who he was referring to. Knowing Paul, it could be anyone. He was always friendly and talked to anyone that acknowledged his presence.

A smile creased her lips as Dinah allowed the words Paul spoke to Cash to sink in. She recalled Paul saying a similar phrase to her every time she spoke to him. He always started with *Life is precious baby, make every day count,* and ended with *I love you today and always.*

"What's wrong, Miss Dinah?" Cash asked looking at Dinah perplexed. "Why are you crying?"

Dinah hadn't realized tears had fallen until Cash pointed them out. "Nothing is wrong, baby. You made me remember something I guess I had forgotten. Thank you for sharing your story about Paul with me. He was my fiancé. We were going to get married, but he's in heaven now."

Cash rose from the floor where he had been kneeling by the coffee table and walked over to Dinah. He put his arms around her and hugged her tight. "It's okay, Miss Dinah. He's in a better place. That's what my grandmama told me when my granddaddy went to heaven. Grandmama said we can't bring nobody back from heaven but we can show them how much we love them by living the best life we can and staying happy. My grandmama always be smiling because she said if we keep smiling and do good, one day we will go to heaven too. That's the reward. You know like when we win a prize at school for doing good."

Placing his hands on each side of Dinah's face, Cash pulled her lips up into a smile. See Miss Dinah, you got to smile like this and be happy so you can get your reward like my grandmama said. I miss Mr. Paul, but I'm glad you're still here. If you wasn't, I don't know what I would have did when I got scared and my mama wasn't home. You're special Miss Dinah and you gone do big things in the world just like Mr. Paul said I was. Now you have to stop crying because you said we can play Uno after we finish our hot chocolate and I don't want you to get the cards wet.

CHAPTER 10

A soft knock on the door interrupted Dinah and Cash's card game. Dinah opened the door to find Cash's mother standing on the other side holding the note Dinah left on her door.

"Cash," she called out with arms extended. Cash ran into her arms showering her with kisses.

Dinah folded her arms ready to give Gina a piece of her mind for leaving Cash alone in the apartment and then showing up so late. Everything in her wanted to let Cash's mother have it, but the more she watched Cash embrace her the more her defenses fell. Cash showed his mother love and adoration as if she had never done anything wrong.

"Get your stuff, baby so we can go home." Gina said to him. She turned to Dinah with apologetic eyes and said, "Thank you for taking care of my baby. I was so scared that I wouldn't make it back home to him. If something would have happened to Cash I don't know what I would have done. I'm sorry for how I treated you the other day. Trust and believe I learned my lesson I won't ever leave him again.

Cash joined his mother at the door. On the way out, he stopped and put his arms around Dinah's legs. "I had so much fun with you, Miss Dinah. Can I come over here again some time?"

Dinah placed her hand on Cash's back. "It's okay with me, if your mama says it's okay."

"Thank you again, Dinah. I'm so glad you were here for Cash. I guess my mama is right. She said God works in mysterious ways and whatever He needs to do to get your attention He will do it. He definitely got my attention. For real, for real."

Closing her apartment door, Dinah kneeled down beside the sofa. She started to pick up the cards she and Cash had been playing with but instead, she closed her eyes and prayed.

Thank you Lord, for answering the prayer I didn't even know I had. Losing Paul has been the hardest thing I have ever endured. I felt like I couldn't go on without him being in my life. I honestly didn't want to live. I didn't see much need in it. I allowed him to be so important to me that I lost sight of who you are to me. My mama says all the time you have a purpose for my life. I struggled to see it. Because I couldn't see it, I took the life you have given me for granted. I know I'm not going to wake up in the morning and automatically be okay. I realize it's a process. Father, please help me through this. Help me to see the reason I'm still here and help me to make every day count. You gave me this life and I promise I will spend the rest of my days showing you my gratitude. Help me to live each day to the fullest, so that when you do get ready for me I can get the reward you have for me in heaven. I stopped celebrating Christmas because I thought without Paul, there was no Christmas. I now realize it's not about Paul. It's not even about me. Father, there is no Christmas without you.

The End

Note From The Author

Thank you so much for taking the time to read *"No Christmas Without You"*. I have been trying to write this story for years, but never understood why such a short story was so hard to complete. Much like Dinah, I had to come to a place within where I realized every stumbling block was meant to distract me from the things God has called me to do. I allowed circumstances, finances and the loss of people very close to me to be my constant excuse.

I often prayed and asked God to help me get over the things I perceived as a loss; so I could move forward, but like a human trying to knock down a house with their bare hands, I found the task impossible. It wasn't until I realized my gift wasn't about me, but it was to be shared to both entertain and offer hope. It was only then that I was able to finally break through the invisible wall.

I know this story is short in length, yet I pray the message is one that will stay with you. One that will be carried forward: to uplift and encourage those who are facing challenges both without and within. My prayer is that God will heal your hurt and erase your scars those visible and those only He can see. May you be blessed during the season that is set aside for Christmas and every day.

I encourage you this day and every day moving forward to LIVE, don't merely exist. Your life has purpose and no matter what it looks like on the outside, things will get better. Your life is worth living. Go forth and make an impact.

Blessings,

LaCricia A'ngelle

About the Author

LaCricia A'ngelle is a licensed Evangelist, Author, and Publisher. A native of Chicago, she currently resides in Alabama with her family.

To arrange signings, book events, speaking engagements, or to send comments to the author please email her at: author@lacriciaangelle.com

Connect with LaCricia A'ngelle online at:
www.lacriciaangelle.com
www.facebook.com/lacriciaangelle or
www.facebook.com/authorlacricia
Twitter: @authorlacricia
Instagram: @lacricia_angelle

Other Books by LaCricia A'ngelle

Girl, Naw!
It Ain't Over
Positive Deception
Lina's Redemption
Journey to Love
Worthy of Love
Sophomore Mom
The Christmas Gift

Your Personal Invitation

Behold, I stand at the door and knock. If anyone hears My voice and opens the door, I will come in to him and dine with him, and he with Me. Romans 3:20 NKJV

As we go through life, we often seek ways to fill void areas in our hearts. Whatever you may be seeking, you can find it in a personal relationship with Jesus Christ.

If you believe God is knocking on the door of your heart, this is your opportunity to welcome Him into your life.

If you have never accepted Jesus Christ as your personal Lord and Savior, I extend to you this invitation.

Check out these awesome reads by
Author LaCricia A'ngelle